WITCHES
of
BROOKLYN
WHAT THE HEX?!

Also by Sophie Escabasse

Witches of Brooklyn

SOPHIE ESCABASSE

WITCHES
of
BROOKLYN
WHAT THE HEX?!

What the Hex?! was drawn with red pencils of all sorts, until they were two and a half inches long. Book 1 was sketched in blue and I wanted to easily differentiate the sketches of book 2. Then all the pages were scanned. Inking and coloring were done with Procreate and Photoshop.

Text, cover art, and interior illustrations copyright © 2021 by Sophie Escabasse
Case art used under license from Shutterstock.com

All rights reserved. Published in the United States by RH Graphic, an imprint of Random House Children's Books, a division of Penguin Random House LLC, New York.

RH Graphic with the book design is a trademark of Penguin Random House LLC.

Visit us on the Web! RHKidsGraphic.com • @RHKidsGraphic

Educators and librarians, for a variety of teaching tools, visit us at RHTeachersLibrarians.com

Library of Congress Cataloging-in-Publication Data is available upon request.
ISBN 978-0-593-11930-3 (pbk.) — ISBN 978-0-593-12544-1 (trade)
ISBN 978-0-593-11931-0 (lib. bdg.) — ISBN 978-0-593-11932-7 (ebk)

Designed by Patrick Crotty

MANUFACTURED IN CHINA
10 9 8 7 6 5 4 3 2
First Edition

A comic on every bookshelf.

For Brooklyn and all my friends over there

Chapter 1

I called three or four times—
she was never there!

And I know her family didn't
go anywhere. I ran into her
brother the other day.

And she never called me back, of course.

I wouldn't worry about Berrit.

Maybe she got a smartphone for Christmas...

That would keep her busy for days and nights... It would probably even prevent her from consuming food!! Her brain would suffocate...

The phone has consumed our friend!!

HA HA HA HA HA

DRIING DRIIINNG DDRII

?

!!

It looks like they're early.

It's my aunts' guests I was telling you about. I'm gonna have to go.

Sorry about the game.

No problem...

5

Old family friends and colleagues.

Selimene and Carlota really want me to meet them.

Knowing your aunts, it won't be a dull tea party.

I'm sure their friends will be pretty interesting!

Oliver the optimist! Hopefully you're right.

You'll be fine, Effie. See you at school!

Okay, let's do this.

C'mon, Effie, they'll like you...there are worse things than meeting some old family friends.

A LOT of family friends.

THE MOON GIRL! I told you the moon...

BLAH BLAH BLAH BLAH BLAH

7

Hem...

Welcome, everyone! As always, it is a real pleasure to have you all here tonight. Thanks for coming to our biannual reunion.

Before we officially start today's meeting, Carlota and I have something important to tell you.

Or I should say, someone important to introduce to you...

Why are my hands prickly, Carlota?

It's because of all the magic in the room, my dear. You're sensing it.

OH.

Magic isn't done surprising you, little one! You'll see.

The secret is to hold the reins, but to let it drive...sometimes.

You'll be just fine. I see it!

Hem. Sure thing, Sissi! Should we move on to our meeting now?

We don't want it to end at the witching hour like last time!

A GHOST?! A-a-a real ghost, like in the movies? A BOO type of ghost?

Ha ha! More or less, my dear, more or less.

The ghost was a lovely lady from Europe who died while she was visiting family in New York. Of course, she couldn't find her way home, poor thing.

I helped her to get back on track.

These things happen more often than we think.

16

C'mon, Sharpy. They're harmless!

I'm not sure it's good for the profession to have all these hobbyists taking center stage!

And they're really nice girls!

Most of them are very eco-friendly...they're respectful—and feminist, obviously. That's good. But I'm afraid there'll be an accident one of these days with the amount of candles they light in their apartments.

About a month ago, weird accidents started to happen on Sixth Avenue.

I didn't pay much attention at first, but the trouble and number of injuries increased, and they were always happening right at the same corner, you see?!

25

WHAAAAT...?

Francis has a big book about the dragons of New York State, if you wish to learn more, my darling.

Anything else we should know about your stormy corner, Sissi? Anything out of the ordinary?

29

30

And the meeting went on...

They're all so different...each one has their own area of expertise. Who knew witches could be teachers...

...choreographers...

34

Oh, and what was the peace circle for, exactly?

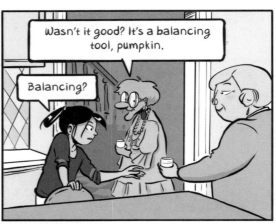

Wasn't it good? It's a balancing tool, pumpkin.

Balancing?

The idea is to generate peaceful energy to counterbalance the city's madness, you see?

There will be a bit less anger in the world tonight.

Whoa... awesome.

Good night, pumpkin. You did well tonight.

Thanks, Selimene. Night!

Chapter 2

TADIN!!

Good morning, sunshine!

Morning, guys! I can't wait to see Berrit and hear what happened to her over the holidays!

Can I finish the chia-seed-and-coconut-milk pudding?

Of course!

45

Ready?

Ready!

So how was the introduction to the family friends?

Pretty fun! You were right, I met some very interesting people... One woman was a hacker! Can you believe that?

What does she hack?

No idea.

46

EFFIE, Oliver! SO HAPPY TO SEE YOU BOTH!

This is Garance!

Hi!

Garance arrived only three weeks ago from France. Can you imagine?! And we're neighbors!! Isn't that awesome?! Her family moved into our building. We had so much fun over the holidays!

Welcome to Brooklyn, Garance. I'm Oliver.

Effie. Hi!

Hi!

It's gonna be so cool, because...

...GUESS WHAT!

WE'RE IN THE SAME CLASS!!!

Isn't that awesome?

It's really nice to already know people in your class...

And we're the BEST people! You'll sit with us! There's a spot at our table.

I hadn't realized you were new too.

I'm not that new.

Everyone, get the book you're studying and go sit with your book group.

Can Garance be in my group, Ms. Pratt?

Sure, you could study the same book for this session. That's a good idea.

YAY!! C'mon! We're sitting with Miles, Agatha, and Vincent! We're reading historical fiction at the moment. Our book's called *The War That Saved My Life.*

Have you been to Paris? Have you seen the Eiffel Tower?

Can you curse in French?

Have you seen a lot of soccer games?

Well, I really wonder what the mother will do when she realizes her daughter is gone...and the horse...

So? How were your holidays, Effie?

Good!! Can I talk to you for a minute? I—

BERRiT!

Would you mind showing me to the bathroom?

OF COURSE! Do you want the closest or the nicest?

Sigh.

Seriously! Can you believe that?

WE WERE TRANSPARENT!!

ALL DAY!

It's like we don't exist anymore!

Don't worry...it's Berrit we're talking about. You know her! She's always overexcited. That's her trademark.

SIGH.

I had a
horrible day,
Lion.

And I don't feel like
studying magic at all...

SIGH

SIGH!

Better go before
Francis gets mad.
See you, Lion.

GOOD AFTERNOON, YOUNG LADY. THANK YOU FOR BEING *ALMOST* ON TIME!

Hi, francis.

HERE YOU GO. SO, DO YOU REMEMBER WHICH PART OF ARIANA'S STRENGTHENING SPELL WE WERE STUDYING LAST TIME?

Mmh...the witches among the suffragettes?

WELL, THAT WAS IN OUR WITCHES' HISTORY CLASS, EFFIE. WE'RE STUDYING SPELLS TODAY. LIKE EVERY MONDAY.

WITCHES' HISTORY IS ON WEDNESDAYS. CAN WE PLEASE FOCUS HERE?

OF COURSE! Ha ha. I knew that, Francis! Hem. The spell...Ariana...Mmh, we were, we were...there was a stone involved, right?

SIGH.

AS WE'VE BEEN STUDYING FOR THE LAST TWO WEEKS...

...THIS STRENGTHENING SPELL IS VERY CONVENIENT BECAUSE OF ITS SIMPLICITY. NO RARE INGREDIENTS ARE NEEDED, NOR...

...MONTHS AND MONTHS OF PREPARATIONS. THE STAGE OF THE DOESN'T MATTER. EVEN IF, URSE A NEW MOON IS ALWAYS ITABLE ... FOR THE REASONS ALL KNOW. IF SOME CHANGES HAVE BEEN MADE TO THE ...

I have to talk to Berrit alone tomorrow. That's the only way.

VLAM!!

?

It didn't go too well, Lion.

Holy pineapple! It's not easy to heal a hypochondriac!

How was your day, sugar puff?

Very...mediocre.

Ouch! We don't like mediocre. What happened?

Did Oliver notice it too?

Of course he did! You couldn't miss it. She was so passionate! But he says that Berrit is always like that...

And do you agree?

I don't know. I don't think I like Garance very much.

Who?

Garance. The new French girl.

If Berrit is good friends with Garance, you may want to make an effort and get to know her better...

Argh.

It sometimes requires patience and understanding.

Friendship isn't always a smooth waltz.

Look at Carlota and me! We're BFFs.

And that definitely helped me decide to switch to the resistance, aka the "Green Side"! Mmm...and no regrets!

Freedom is essential in any relationship, Effie. We don't own people. Even our best friend!

BFF, Carlota. BFF!

65

Just give it some time, tiger! It will all fall into place.

MMH.

DRING! DRING!

I overslept! I HAVE TO GO!

Here is your bag. Food's inside!

THANK YOU!

LOVE YOU GUYS!

C'mon, Effie! Patience and understanding! You can do that! Piece of cake!

Piece of cake.

Hi, Effie!

Hi!

I could SO eat ten of your mother's Italian Christmas cakes right now!!

Ah...those are so good!

Have you tried them, Effie?

No...

I'll bring you some next time my mom bakes them.

Wednesday

Patience, under-standing, patience. I can do this!

Thursday

Patience, patience, patience, ...

I can do this!

HA-HA-HA

69

VLAM!!

AAARGH

?

I CAN'T TAKE IT ANYMORE, SELIMENE!! THAT FRENCH GIRL IS RUINING MY LIFE!

NEW

Let's not go full-on dramatic and jump to conclusions, tiger. And put that boot back on! You're coming to Park Slope with me.

We'll go meet Sissi and check that building she mentioned.

71

The grout's gonna dry. It's a shame...

Effie will finish your backsplash! Right, pumpkin?! That'll be amusing. AND I'LL DEAL WITH THE FIRE!!

WHAaa?

Don't worry about the fire, Selimene! It's enchanted. It won't burn anything that's in the house!

YOUR house may be immune, but the neighbors' houses AREN'T!!

And I'm not taking anybody just for the sake of having an apprentice! Now, let's not waste any more time and get to work!

SIGH.

All right...you stubborn nanny goat!

GASP!

Thank you, little one.

Of course! Happy to help.

A sitting female figure, approximately five feet tall, with, indeed, bunny ears. Very colorful...

...orange, blue, yellow. The influence of Niki de Saint Phalle is obvious in the—

Mmh...

What is it, Selimene?

Let's check the building across the street, Sissi! Turn off your duck!

?

It isn't a duck but a goose, Selimene, and she's very knowledgeable in art history...what did you find?

This.

Are you still in touch with the captain of the nearby police station, Sissi?

Robert? Sure! I'll give him a call.

How was it?

We've got a lead!

Two statues.

84

Chapter 3

What are the chances Garance would have vanished overnight, you think?

The chances are pretty low, but...it's friday! No magic practice this afternoon. You can play with your friends!

It's supposed to snow a lot tonight! It's gonna be perfect for sledding tomorrow.

Cool!

We should go to the park.

Sounds good to me.

It's frrviiiiday!! We have art class first period!

Life is beautiful!!

Take your seats, my little artists! I've got a surprise for you today! We'll paint a bouquet in watercolor!

Watercolor is a beautiful technique that allows us to create amazing effects! See the gorgeous paper in front of you? We all start by drawing our bouquet lightly with our pencils.

WHOA!

?

OOH!

WHOA!

DDDRRRiiiiiiNNG!!

Have a great weekend! And don't forget to read!

Hey, Effie! Would you like to come hang out at my place this afternoon?

We could listen to music and eat my mom's cookies...

...with Garance.

Everything all right, Effie? You aren't meeting with your friends this afternoon?

?!

AARGh

?

PoM PoM PoM PoM

?

95

96

Mmh...your waffles are pristine, cupcake!

Thanks! It's Martin's recipe.*

Very well executed! Any plans for today, Effie?

I'm gonna start looking for a new school!

WHAT?

* See book one.

Is that because of this French girl? Effie, honey, leaving isn't a solution! It's avoiding the problem.

Well, then, SO BE IT! I avoid the problem!

And what about your friends? Oliver, Berrit? What about them?

Berrit doesn't seem to want to be my friend, anyway...and I'll make new friends!

Nonsense, sugar puff! You will feel terrible if you do that. Do you remember what we said about friendship?

But I've been understanding and patient!!!

Effie?

Hi, Berrit.

Hi! YOU OKAY?!

MMH..

Listen, would you like to come sledding with us at Prospect Park later this morning?

MMH..

It will be epic! There's so much snow! Oliver will be there, and my brother, and... Garance too.

...

YAY! You made it!

I'm happy you came, Effie.

Yeah...me too.

Pfff!! How many times did we come up and down? I can't feel my legs anymore! It reminds me of the time I raced to the top of the Eiffel Tower with my cousin.

You're so lucky to have lived in Paris. That's my dream destination!

105

Paris is pretty neat, but there's a lot to see in France other than Paris!

If we're going to France together, I'm taking you to Dordogne! And to the Basque Country! And...

I like macarons.

We're talking about delicious desserts, Berrit! The crème de la crème!

This conversation is making me so hungry!

SPIRITS

COMMUNITY BOOKSTORE

Let's cross. It'll be faster that way.

Noo...we're gonna have to walk one more block.

LOCAL ACCESS ONLY

Street closed

SIDEWALK CLOSED

The Stormy Corner.

HAPPY

I'm going in! C'mon, guys! Who's with me?

What?

There's no way I'm doing this!

I forgive you, Garance. It never snows this much in Paris! How would you know how to handle it?

110

My...my arm. I can't move it...it's so painful...

You're...you're gonna be okay.

Let's get you out of here.

AAAAh Ah! SOB

It hurts SO MUCH... SOB.

Berrit! What happened?

OH NO!

I fell...Sob. I hurt my arm badly. I can't move it anymore. Sob.

I'm calling a car. I'm taking you to the ER! Mom's gonna be so mad.

You're gonna be okay, Berrit. Take my scarf to support your arm.

Let's go! I'll call Mom when we're on our way!

Do you want me to come?

Thank you, guys. I'd prefer not. We'll call you when we know more. Get home safely!

I bet you're real proud of the way you handle snow now, genius!

C'mon.

Let's go home before we catch pneumonia. We'll call Berrit's parents in a little while. She'll be fine.

I...I think I need to walk a little bit. I'm sorry. You go ahead.

You sure?

Certain. I'll call you later.

Chapter 4

Hi, Lion.

I guess...

...Selimene and Carlota are still at Sissi's...

Sigh.

Aunt Ma? The...

...the...

...the bonsai!

Ha ha ha...yes. The bonsai. Let's say that this little tree is my retirement form.

Retirement form?

A witch can live a very long life, you see. One hundred and sixty, one hundred and eighty years on average...and let me tell you that after turning one hundred, a human body isn't the most comfortable vehicle to live in!

So you turned into...a tree?

Yes. It is pretty common among talented witches— sorry for the self-congratulations...

—to transfer their souls into trees.

But I've never been into deep dark woods myself. So I figured a bonsai would be perfect!

I enjoy the buoyancy of people's energies around me and following the frantic pace of their lives from the serene and peaceful form of a tree.

Whoa.

"Whoa" indeed. Being a tree is the best way to be one with the universe.

But enough about me! You're the young witch Effie, right?

Yes...

I knew I heard some voices... I can't believe my eyes! Aunt Ma! I thought you were done with the apparition?!

!

It's nice to see you. It has been so long...

Effie...are you all right?

Okay...let's start at the beginning, honey.

Sigh...So, I met everyone at the park, and it was fine at first. We sledded for a while...but Garance kept hogging Berrit... talking about France ALL THE TIME! So when we left the park to go get hot cocoa, I had the idea...

Keep going.

...And then, they left for the ER.

I feel like the worst person in the world!

You certainly aren't, Effie. I'm not impressed by what you did this afternoon, but we all make mistakes. Now let's think what we can learn from there.

You know, a good place to start when you have strong feelings like these and you feel distressed is to talk about it.

Ideally you would talk to the people you have an issue with. In our case, Berrit and Garance...

Don't frown!

Talking about a problem is like opening the window of a stinky room.

You bring in some fresh air! You diffuse the stinkiness.

If you cannot talk to Berrit and Garance just yet, talk to a friend! I'm sure you would have felt some relief if you had talked to Oliver this afternoon...and it may have stopped you from convincing your friends to brave the Stormy Corner.

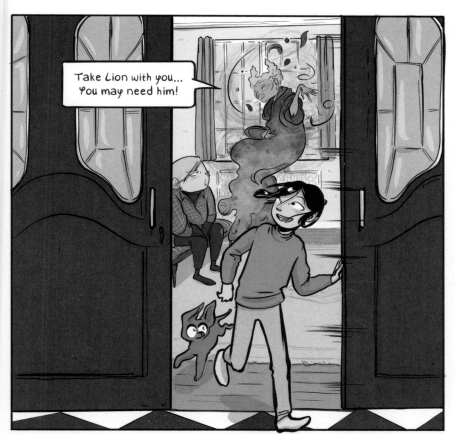

Take Lion with you... You may need him!

Well...goodbye, everyone. Sigh. I guess I'll go prepare my peaceful charm...

SIGH.

FRRRR·······

Almost there, Lion.

Argh...not again! My hands are back to feeling prickly... Could...?

Could it be...?

?

But... but it is...

GARANCE!

What is she doing here?

GASP !

!?!

Were you **REALLY** about to steal that money?!

AAAH!!

I can't believe you were stealing that money!! **GARANCE!**

Effie!! You almost killed me!!

Did...did YOU do that thing with the poster?!

Yes, I'm good with these sorts of things...but that's not the point!!

YOU HAVE POWERS!

You-YOU HAVE MAGIC LIKE I DO!

Yes, but I don't use it to rob people!!

WHY WOULD YOU DO THAT, GARANCE? THERE ARE TONS OF OTHER WAYS TO GET MONEY!!

147

And WHY were you stealing money?!

"All french and interesting"?

The money?

Argh!! To buy a plane ticket!! Are you happy now?!

And it wasn't always stealing! I sold some of my things too. I never wanted to come here! I wanted to stay with my grandmother in the South of France.

She's the only one who knows about my powers. I thought something was wrong with me when they appeared two years ago...

She helped me. She's the only one who understands me! And I have to go back to her!

I almost have all the money!

Wha...what?

But how much have you...?

I told you! Some of that money I earned by selling my things! And I would love to know what you would have done in my position!

I don't know, but...

* See book one

PURR RR...

I swear, I had no idea he could do that.

Purr...

I'm sorry he scared you.

Are you kidding? I'm glad he was here!!

But it may not fly with my mom if we bring him upstairs...

What was it that you wanted me to draw again?

Could you come with me to Park Slope to meet my aunts?

You could make the drawing over there, and I'll explain in the train.

The train... really?

Oh boy...

Well, we can't stay here either. If someone comes by...

Okay, let's not panic...we can put your lion in the bike room...and I'll go ask my mom if I can go to your house.

We've got this, Effie.

You're right...we've got this!

Witches have each other's backs.

Thank you, Garance.

I'll go tell my mom and grab my sketchbook and pencils.

And I'll call my aunts to ask them about Lion.

Everything all right, pumpkin?!

Well... yes...sort of, yes.

Okay, now I'm worried! What's going on?

ARE YOU HURT?!

No, no, I'm fine. But Lion... well, Lion is... He's a lion! A big, enormous lion, and...

WHAT?!

159

Are you Effie?

Y-yes.

Well, c'mon in! We don't have all night, and Selimene is in one of her moods!

And please...

...keep your beast's claws away from my seats, all right?!

HA HA HA HO HO

164

Chapter 5

We're here!

Good luck, kiddos.

Thank you!

You got it, kid.
Stay out of trouble.

Ready to meet the crew?

Ready!

You'll see—they're not usual grandmas...

VLAM

PUMPKIN!

Are you sure you aren't hurt?!

HAPPY

I swear, Selimene, I'm fine!

Open your mouth.

NO WAY!! I'M FINE!

And you're feeling all right as well, my dear?

Yes, thank you. I'm Garance.

But...!

You're...I mean...

FOR CRYING OUT LOUD!! Get inside before anyone sees you! Even I can see that lion!!

To the living room, kids. On your right!

Mmh...a good heart, strong-willed, courageous, proud as an old goat. I respect that...

The descendant of Annabelle Champagnat-Lacroix. That's you! Ha ha!

Something must have gone wrong with my prediction. I wasn't expecting you till spring.

...

Bbz   Bbbzz

Annabelle Champagnat-Lacroix. My grandmother's sister? You knew her?

Indeed! We took a seminar together and became very good friends...

Of course, that was a century ago! Ha ha.

Well, I'll be happy to take you as an apprentice. If you can come here three times a week, I believe that should cover the basics...

Sissi!! You secretive nanny goat!! I CAN'T BELIEVE MY EARS!!

Wai... WAIT! Wait a second!

You—you're offering to...to teach me? To teach me what? To—to be a...

TO BE A WITCH!!

OH, *GUYS*!! I must tell you! Garance can make objects fly!! And her drawings are magic too!

No, they're not.

That reminds me!

I have something Annabelle trusted me to pass along to you. I dug it out of the attic the other day.

It must be on the table behind us.

178

Open it!

It opens?

It sure does. But it wasn't for me, or anybody else, to open. Only you should be able to.

Neat!

WHOA!
A pencil!

Okay...

So my idea is...and it's you, Carlota, who gave it to me when you told me how we have to give words the chance to work for us.

Well, these statues never had that chance.

It's true that, as far as we know, these two never talked.

Exactly! So I thought if Garance could draw them, very realistic, side by side on the same paper...

You would bring the drawing to life.

Yes! And I'll introduce them...and...make them talk to each other!

The idea is good, but you'll have to be on-site.

That's what worries...

POOF!!!

Oh, here you are!!

As I was saying...we'll have to make sure Effie remains safe during the introduction process.

Garance will help keep her safe through the introduction, right, Garance?

That will be good hands-on practice.

You—you're sure?

We'll be there too. We can hold a shield charm.

It's a good plan! It will work. Let's start moving, soldiers!

She was generous when she said "old." This thing is ancient!

At least it turned on.

Here it is.

Do you think you could draw this?

Fingers in the nose! Can you show me the other statue?

Fingers in what?!

French expression...

So how's the new generation doing? Are we good to go?

Almost!

Well done, princess! You are talented, no doubt!

Very nice!

Line drawing
extremely we
executed. Th
statues look
alive...

I'm getting ready to murder our friend!

Argh...we don't have time for this! Night is falling! Let's go!

201

Yes, we don't know each other.

Well, not yet...

But...it kinda always starts that way... there's always the awkward moment when you have to break the ice...

But soon, you won't be able to imagine the place without this friendly face...

...who always has a smile for you when you pass by.

Fifteen minutes later.

It was a pleasure to meet you, young witch.

Likewise.

Please come see us again.

ΨΑΨ!

You did it, honey!!!

What a day! Do you guys do that every weekend?

HA HA HA!!

We're only witches, child. Not the Avengers!

Well, that was awesome!

I'm happy with your performance tonight, Garance. It's too late to talk more about your apprenticeship now...

... but I'll come meet with your parents in a couple of days.

You sure...?

I can tell you're skeptical.

But you'll see! Your parents will LOVE me!

Good night, everyone! Congrats again on the good work!!

Bye, Sissi! See you in Ditmas!

C'mon, ladies! Our flying carpet is here!

Thank you for coming back, Jaz. You're a prince.

Here we are!

Look! It's Berrit and her mom. They must be coming back from the hospital.

We should go say hi.

C'mon!

!

!

Mamma mia!! It's not my arm but my head that I've injured! I'm having a hallucination!!

What kind of magic happened for you two to end up arm in arm?!

Ha ha! A strong kind, Berrit!

How do you feel?

I'm fine. It doesn't hurt anymore.

And look how awesome that is!

Everyone's gonna pamper me now! It's gonna be awesome!

And...

...and it really wasn't cool of me not to return your calls over the holidays...

HA HA HA!!

I would have been super mad at myself!

Epilogue

Purrr
Purrr...

Acknowledgments

Again and again, I want to thank Kelly Sonnack, my extraordinary agent. Thank you for being such an exceptional woman and always standing by my side (rain or shine, worldwide pandemic or not). I am so grateful to be on this adventure with you.

Shout-out to the incredible Random House team, without whom this book wouldn't exist: Gina Gagliano, my editor Whitney Leopard, my designer Patrick Crotty, and Nicole Valdez. Thank you for your hard work shaping today's graphic novel landscape. I am very proud that the Witches of Brooklyn are Random House books, and I can't wait to discover the next graphic novels that'll come out of your magical hats!

Extra-special thanks to my husband, Patrick Flynn, and our children, Ella, Josephine, and Arthur, for being so supportive and enthusiastic about my work.

A BIG thank-you to Ariane for sticking with my crazy family during all the challenges that 2020 threw at us. Choupette, your work with the raccoons made this book possible.

Thank you to my family in France, who showed me so much support and sent me tons of love vibes over the ocean.

Thank you to all the readers who enjoyed *Witches of Brooklyn*. Your nice words brought butterflies to my stomach and made my pencils fly real high!

Finally, thank you to the magical booksellers and librarians who helped and supported the witches. ♡

Sophie Escabasse is a french-born illustrator and comic artist. A Brooklynite at heart, she's now living in Montreal with her husband, their three children, and her old black cat.

Originally trained as a graphic designer, she worked in advertising in Paris and New York City before fully embracing illustration as her career. Her work has appeared in the Derby Daredevils series by Kit Rosewater. Hailing from a family of graphic novel lovers, Sophie has been enjoying comics since she could read. Becoming a graphic novel author has been her lifelong dream, and today she's happily juggling being a mother of three and a comic artist of a new trilogy.

It's a lot of sweat but a lot of fun!

esofii.com
⌾ esofiii

Sophie's Sketchbook

Garance

Her dad comes
from Madagascar
She used to live
in Marseille.
Then Paris before
moving to
Brooklyn.

Sophie's Sketchbook

05:AM

Sophie's Sketchbook

Option 1.
Face in keystone.
above door.

Option II
Bas-relief

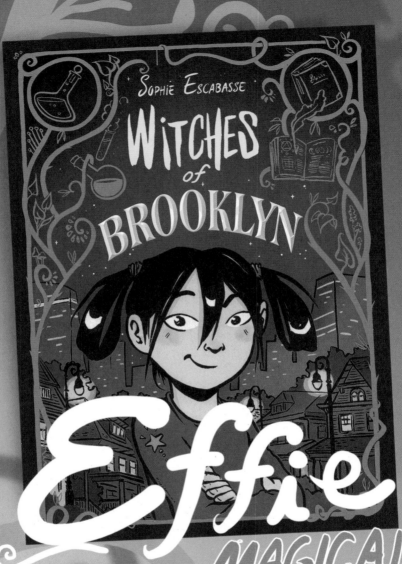

Sophie Escabasse

Witches of Brooklyn

Effie

and her MAGICAL adventures continue in 2022!

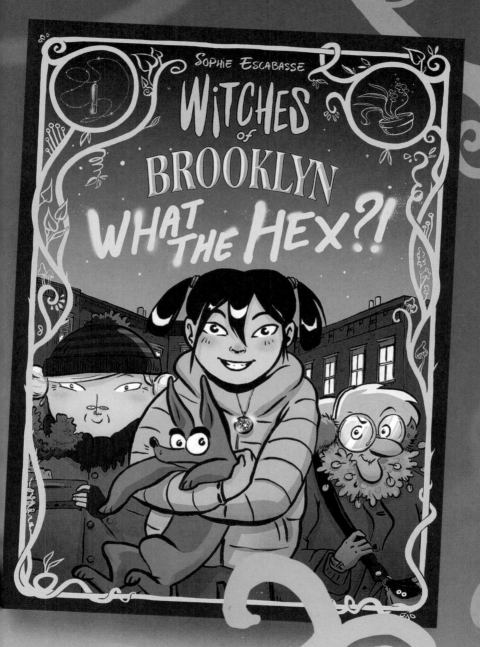

MAGIC AND ADVENTURE AWAIT
in these must-read
GRAPHIC NOVELS